Fred Korematsu

CHERRY LAKE PRESS

Published in the United States of America by Cherry Lake Publishing Group
Ann Arbor, Michigan
www.cherrylakepublishing.com

Reading Adviser: Beth Walker Gambro, MS, Ed., Reading Consultant, Yorkville, IL
Book Designer: Jennifer Wahi
Illustrator: Jeff Bane

Photo Credits: © Fred T. Korematsu Institute, 5; © Natee K Jindakum/Shutterstock, 7 © mikeljay1968/Shutterstock, 9; © Everett Collection/Shutterstock, 11; © Library of Congress/LOC No. 2001697374/Photo by Clem Albers, 13, 22; © Library of Congress/LOC No. 2002695984/Photo by Ansel Adams, 15; © MR.Yanukit/Shutterstock, 17; © Vitalii Vodolazskyi/Shutterstock, 19, 23; © Fred T. Korematsu Institute, 21; Jeff Bane, Cover, 1, 8, 12, 18; Various frames throughout, Shutterstock images

Library of Congress Cataloging-in-Publication Data

Names: Loh-Hagan, Virginia, author. | Bane, Jeff, 1957- illustrator.
Title: Fred Korematsu / by Virginia Loh-Hagan ; illustrator, Jeff Bane.
Description: Ann Arbor, Michigan : Cherry Lake Publishing Group, [2022] | Series: My itty-bitty bio | Audience: Grades K-1
Identifiers: LCCN 2021036535 (print) | LCCN 2021036536 (ebook) | ISBN 9781534198982 (hardcover) | ISBN 9781668900123 (paperback) | ISBN 9781668901564 (pdf) | ISBN 9781668905883 (ebook)
Subjects: LCSH: Korematsu, Fred, 1919-2005--Juvenile literature. | Japanese Americans--Evacuation and relocation, 1942-1945--Juvenile literature. | Japanese Americans--Civil rights--History--20th century--Juvenile literature. | Civil rights workers--United States--Biography--Juvenile literature. | Japanese Americans--Biography--Juvenile literature. | Korematsu, Fred, 1919-2005--Trials, litigation, etc.--Juvenile literature.
Classification: LCC D769.8.A6 K675 2019 (print) | LCC D769.8.A6 (ebook) | DDC 341.6/7 [B]--dc23
LC record available at https://lccn.loc.gov/2021036535
LC ebook record available at https://lccn.loc.gov/2021036536

Printed in the United States of America
Corporate Graphics

About the author: When not writing, Dr. Virginia Loh-Hagan serves as the director of the Asian Pacific Islander Desi American (APIDA) Resource Center at San Diego State University. She identifies as Chinese American and is committed to amplifying APIDA communities. She lives in San Diego with her very tall husband and very naughty dogs.

About the illustrator: Jeff Bane and his two business partners own a studio along the American River in Folsom, California, home of the 1849 Gold Rush. When Jeff's not sketching or illustrating for clients, he's either swimming or kayaking in the river to relax.

My parents were **immigrants** from Japan. They moved to the United States in 1905. I was born in 1919.

I grew up with three brothers.
We lived in California.

I played sports in school. I was on the swim and tennis teams.

What do you like to do at school?

Japan attacked Hawaii in 1941. The United States entered World War II. I wanted to help. But I was Japanese. People saw me as the enemy.

A law was passed. It targeted Japanese Americans. The law was unfair. My **rights** were taken away.

Japanese Americans were sent to **internment camps**. These camps were like jails. My family went. But I didn't. I fought back. I wanted to change the law. I went to the **Supreme Court**. I lost.

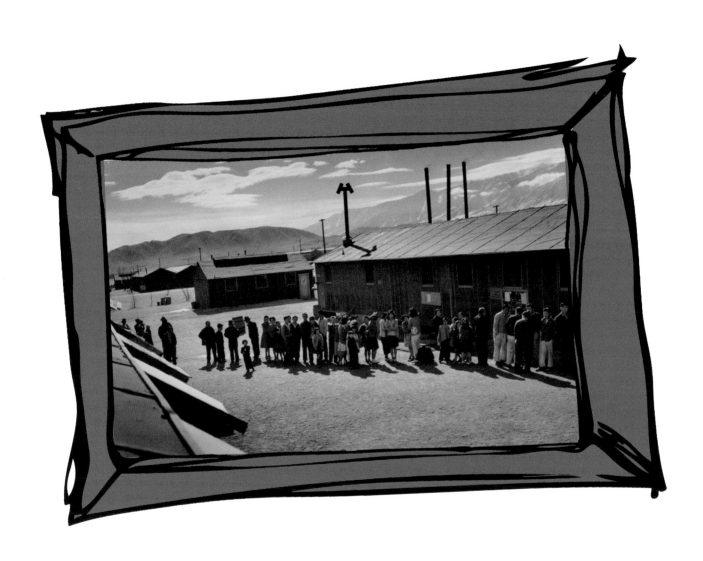

I did not stop. I spoke up. I went back to court.

What do you speak up against?

Years later, I won. A court in California said the law was unfair.

I received the **Presidential Medal of Freedom** in 1998. I died in 2005. But my **legacy** lives on. I fought for **civil rights**.

What would you like to ask me?

1942

1910

Born
1919

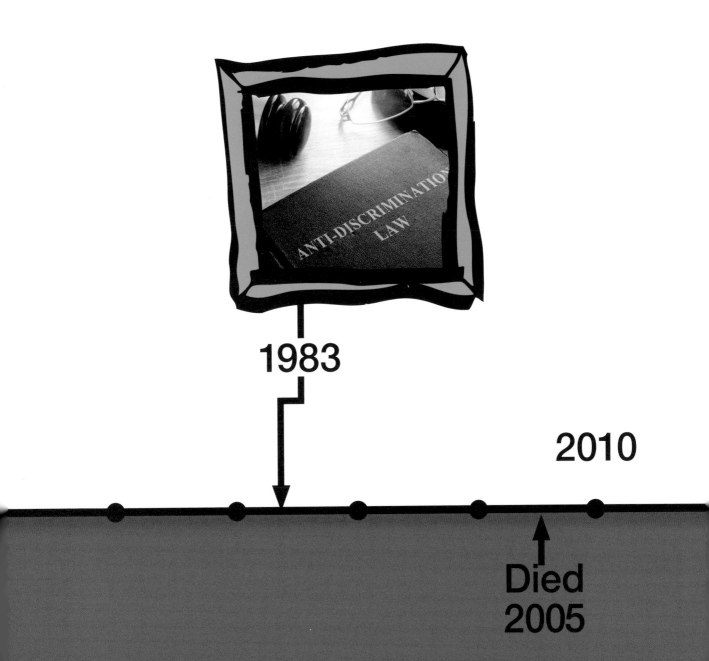

1983

2010

Died
2005

glossary

civil rights (SIH-vuhl RITES) the rights of citizens to political and social freedom and equality

immigrants (IH-muh-gruhnts) people who leave one country to live permanently in another

internment camps (in-TUHRN-muhnt KAMPS) prisons where people are held during war

legacy (LEH-guh-see) something handed down from one generation to another

Presidential Medal of Freedom (preh-zuh-DEN-shuhl MEH-duhl UHV FREE-duhm) the highest civilian honor a person in the United States can receive

rights (RITES) things to which people are entitled by law

Supreme Court (suh-PREEM KORT) the highest court in the United States

index